P9-DTW-856

Braving the Storm

Written by Maria Grace Dateno, FSP

Illustrated by Paul Cunningham

Pauline
BOOKS & MEDIA
Boston

Library of Congress Cataloging-in-Publication Data

Dateno, Maria Grace.
  Braving the storm / written by Maria Grace Dateno ; illustrated by Paul
Cunningham.
      p. cm. -- (Gospel time trekkers ; [#2])
  Summary: Siblings Hannah, Caleb, and Noah, aged six through ten,
travel through time and space to Cana, where they hear about Jesus's
first miracle, as well as the miracle of the loaves and fishes.
  ISBN-13: 978-0-8198-1204-9
  ISBN-10: 0-8198-1204-8
  [1. Space and time--Fiction. 2. Brothers and sisters--Fiction. 3. Turning
water into wine at the wedding at Cana (Miracle)--Fiction. 4. Feeding of
the five thousand (Miracle)--Fiction. 5. Jesus Christ--Miracles--Fiction. 6.
Christian life--Fiction.] I. Cunningham, Paul, (Paul David), 1972- ill. II.
Title.
  PZ7.D2598Br 2013
  [Fic]--dc23
                                      2012029876

The Scripture quotations contained herein are from the *New Revised Standard Version Bible: Catholic Edition*, copyright © 1989, 1993, Division of Christian Education of the National Council of the Churches of Christ in the United States of America. Used by permission. All rights reserved.

Cover design by Mary Joseph Peterson, FSP

Cover and interior art by Paul Cunningham

Published by Pauline Books & Media, 50 Saint Pauls Avenue, Boston, MA 02130-3491

Printed in the U.S.A.

BTS KSEUSAHUDNHA2-261043 1204-8

www.pauline.org

Pauline Books & Media is the publishing house of the Daughters of St. Paul, an international congregation of women religious serving the Church with the communications media.

3 4 5 6 7 8 9   18 17 16 15

To my mom and dad,
with love and gratitude.

Contents

Chapter One

An Idea That Works

This adventure happened on a hot Saturday in June. The day started off great. Then it got terrible. Then it got great again.

Right after breakfast, I went with my dad to his workshop. I was so excited. His workshop is where he makes toys and furniture out of wood, which is his job. I had been asking him for a month to teach me what he does. And he had promised that today we would start.

The workshop has a lot of light because of the big windows. And there's always the smell of fresh wood shavings. I like sweeping them up and putting them in the big barrel.

"What are we going to make, Dad?" I asked as we put on the denim coveralls. (Mom says they're aprons, but Dad calls them coveralls.)

"Well, we might not get as far as making things today, Caleb. There's a lot of basic stuff to learn before you start handling the saw and cutting the wood."

"Yeah, but I learn fast, right, Dad?"

"We'll see how far we get."

I should have realized when he said this that we weren't going to get very far at all. Dad wanted to go through all these rules about safety and then just sit there and talk about the wood and look at it. I wanted to cut it or at least sand it. I wanted to make something!

Anyway, that's when the day became terrible. I said I was bored. And then Dad said maybe I was too young to learn woodworking. So I got mad and left.

It was very hot outside, but I didn't want to go into the house. My mom would ask why I was done so soon. So I walked over to our weeping willow tree, thinking I could sit in the shade and hide for a while.

My older sister Hannah was there already, reading. She's almost eleven and always has her nose in a book. She didn't even look up when I pushed aside the hanging branches and sat down next to her.

"Hi, Hannah," I said.

"Hi," she replied, still not looking up.

"Want to do something?"

"No, I want to read my book," she said.

"Come on, Hannah. Let's do something fun."

"I want to read, Caleb. Why don't you do something with Noah?"

Noah is my six-year-old brother.

"Noah can come, too," I said. "In fact, he has to. We need him, to do what I'm planning."

Now Hannah looked up.

"What do you mean?" she asked. "What are you planning?"

"I want to go *there* again, Hannah."

"Go where?"

"*You* know," I said. "Go back in time, to the time of Jesus."

Now you may think that was a funny thing for me to say, but it actually had happened before. Hannah, Noah, and I were riding our bikes down the hill together and had found ourselves in another place and time.

It had been so much fun, and I really, *really* wanted it to happen again.

Hannah sighed and rolled her eyes.

"Caleb, listen to me. There's no way for us to 'go there.' There's no way to *make* it happen. It just happened before. It may or may not happen again."

But I was certain she was wrong. I was sure we could do it again if we only figured out what we did that made it happen before.

The one thing we did agree on was that we couldn't do exactly what we had done the first time. We had already tried riding our bikes down the hill again. It didn't work.

"There must be some way to figure it out!" I said.

"There *isn't*, Caleb," she said. "We just have to wait to see if it happens."

"I have an idea," I said, getting up. "I'm going to get Noah so we can try it out."

"No more trying things out," said Hannah. "I told you it won't work!"

Noah came out the back door at that moment.

"Noah, come over here!" I called.

When he had arrived, I said, "Just listen. I've been thinking. When it happened before, the three of us were together, riding our bikes down the hill."

"We already tried that!" said Hannah. "How many times did we ride down that stupid hill! You wanted to try it at different times of the day, different days of the week. It didn't work!"

"But don't you see? That was because it can't work exactly the same way twice." I took a breath. "I think what made it work was that we were all together, moving in a downward motion. Let's climb up on that branch and jump down together."

"Yeah, let's try it!" said Noah. He looked as excited as I felt.

"No, you guys! I am going to sit here and read. I am not climbing up the tree. I'm too hot, and it *won't* work," said Hannah.

"Please?" I asked.

"No, try it yourselves!"

"No, Hannah, it has to be all three of us. I'm sure of that," I said.

"Please!" said Noah with his eyes wide and pleading. "I want to go back there and see Jesus!"

"Oh, all *right*," said Hannah, "but it's not going to work."

She got up with a groan, and we climbed up into the old willow. The first branch is low, so even Noah could get up on it.

"Okay, now!" I yelled, and we all jumped together. We fell in slow motion, as if the air had become as thick as water, and landed with a gentle thud. I looked down at my tan-colored tunic.

"Yes!" I cried. "It worked!"

Chapter Two

Finding the Way

Hannah and Noah looked at their clothes. We had on the same tunics as last time. They were like robes that had a belt made from rope tied around the waist.

Noah started whooping with joy and jumping up and down. Hannah just stood there with her mouth open. I smiled at her.

"I told you so!"

Hannah rolled her eyes. "Okay, you were right. It worked. I can't see how jumping out of a tree can make a person go back in time, but somehow it did."

"We didn't have these last time," said Noah. We all had large scarves around our shoulders.

"It seems a little cooler now," said Hannah.

"Maybe it's a different time of year," I said. "Maybe Benjamin is back from the place they were taking the sheep last time we came."

Benjamin was the shepherd boy we had met last time, along with his father and his grandfather. Eldad, the grandfather, was one of the shepherds who had seen the angels when Jesus was born. It was so *neat* to hear him tell the story!

"The last time we came was only about a month ago," said Hannah.

"In *our* time, yes," I said, "but last time, when we were here for two days, no time at all passed at home. So who knows how much time has gone by now?"

"Come on, let's go—there's the town!" said Noah. "Let's see if Benjamin is home!"

We were much closer to the town than the last time we came, so it only took a few minutes to walk there. We didn't see any sheep or shepherds, but we did see rows of old trees lined up on the hill. It looked a little like the apple orchard our neighbors have.

"I don't remember these trees. And I don't see the stables that Benjamin showed us. Maybe we're on the other side of the town," I said.

We walked into the town until we came to an open area. There were a lot of people.

"It looks like this is the marketplace," said Hannah.

"What are they selling?" said Noah, pointing to a table. "I want to see what's in those jars! We could get one for Mom."

"We don't have any money, remember, Noah?" said Hannah.

"Look at that!" said Noah. "What is that man doing?"

"Don't run off, Noah. We need to stick together," said Hannah.

"Can we go see what is on that table? Why are we just standing here?"

"Hold your horses, Noah!" said Hannah. I smiled because she sounded like Mom talking to Noah in the grocery store.

"I have an idea," I said, trying to get Noah's attention. "Let's ask someone the way to the stables on the edge of town. Then from there we can find the street that Benjamin said his family lives on."

"That sounds good," said Hannah.

"Yeah!" said Noah.

We looked around at the people in the marketplace. Most of them seemed to be setting up their stuff to sell. There weren't very many people who were looking at the things like they were shopping. Hannah wanted to wait until we saw a mom with her children. But I saw a man nearby, putting small pots and other metal objects on a cloth on the ground. He looked nice, so I went over to him.

"Good morning, sir," I said. "Could you help us find the stables?"

"The stables?" he asked, looking up from arranging things on the cloth. "Do you mean the ones by the inn?" He pointed across the open area of the market toward a building nearby.

"No, the stables on the side of town where the sheep are."

"I do not know of any sheep or stables, son. I am a merchant; I come every so often to sell my small metal goods and the kinds of spices that are not available here in Galilee."

"Do you know a boy named Benjamin?" asked Noah.

"No, child, the only boy I know here is Levi, my son. He ran off to gather the news of the town. We arrived late last night. But are you lost? I can help you find your relatives. I surely would want someone to help my son if he were lost in a town he had never been to."

"Well, thank you for your offer," said Hannah, "but we've been to Bethlehem before. And we don't have any relatives here, only friends."

"Bethlehem?" asked the man. "You truly are very lost. We are a long way from Bethlehem. This town is called Sogane."

Chapter Three

Good News

We stood there and stared at the man. I was wondering if he was teasing us, but his face didn't look like it.

"So . . . how far is it to Bethlehem?" asked Hannah after several seconds.

The man laughed a little. "It's quite a long way. You head south and go past a lot of little towns in Galilee, through the open country, into Samaria. After that, you will see Jerusalem before you come to Bethlehem. Why do you want to go there?"

Just then a boy came running up. He had straight dark brown hair, like the man, and a nice tunic with white and reddish-brown stripes on it. He was smiling.

"Abba! Abba! I have news!"

We knew from our last adventure that "Abba" was what children around here called their dads.

"This is my son, Levi," said the man. "What are your names?"

"I'm Hannah, and these are my brothers Caleb and Noah."

"Levi? You mean like the kind of jeans?" asked Noah.

"What?" Levi and his dad said at the same time.

"Nothing, never mind," I said.

"Anyway," said Levi, "I have to tell you my news. The people I talked to said they will be going out to the countryside near Jotapata because they heard Jesus was going to be there!"

"Jesus?" I asked. "Where?"

"We want to see him!" said Noah.

"Are you going?" asked Hannah. "Can we come with you?"

"I thought you three were going to Bethlehem," said Levi's dad.

"Well, last time we were here, it *was* Bethlehem," said Noah. "So we thought we were there this time, too."

"What?" said Levi.

"Nothing, never mind," said Hannah. "Can you tell us where Jotapata is, so we can go see Jesus?"

"So, can I go, Abba?" asked Levi. "You promised that next time we were in Galilee and we heard he was nearby, I could go see him again."

"Well," said his dad, "I guess you can go. If there are a lot of people going out to Jotapata, that explains why the market is so quiet today. I can take care of any buyers who come."

"Yay! Thank you, Abba!"

"Here are some coins for you to get provisions. If you do find Jesus where they say, you can continue to Jotapata and ask for Simon the coppersmith's house and stay with him. I will be there tomorrow."

"Okay," said Levi.

"And if you go out there and don't find him, then be back here by sunset. And take the brown mantle because it looks like rain."

"Okay," said Levi, taking the large scarf that his father handed him.

"And remember what I have taught you about reading the sky—watch the clouds and the sun so that you do not get lost."

"Okay," said Levi again.

"And remember what I have taught you about drinking from the streams."

"Okay, Abba," said Levi. "I will remember everything. See you tomorrow!"

"Let's go!" said Noah.

We went with Levi toward a small building on the edge of the marketplace.

"Are you going to go back to wherever you are staying to get some provisions?" asked Levi. "You do not need to bring water because there are a lot of streams around here."

We looked at each other. "We don't have any money," said Noah.

"Oh?" said Levi. "Well, that is all right. I will get enough bread and cheese and figs for all of us."

"Thank you, Levi," said Hannah. "That is very kind of you."

"Oh, I am always glad to share!" said Levi, and he laughed as if sharing was something really fun.

Chapter Four

Off to Jotapata

Levi put the food he had bought into a bag he carried over his shoulder. Then we walked down the street and out through the main gates of the town.

"Levi," I said, "you said you wanted to go see Jesus 'again.' When did you see him before?"

"It was the last time we were in this area of Galilee, not far from here. You see, I have just begun to accompany my father on his longer trips. My mother and my older sister are at home with my younger brothers and sisters. My family lives in Bethany."

"That's near Jerusalem, right?" said Hannah. I was surprised she knew something like that. It must be in the Bible.

"No, this Bethany is across the Jordan in Perea," said Levi.

"Oh, I have never heard of that one."

"Well, my father and I are away for a week or more at a time. We bring mostly metal goods—like small copper pots and jugs—that are very well made. Most towns have some metal goods available, but the items that we bring are harder to find. Also, we have spices traded from the East. We get them in the Decapolis." Levi sounded very proud of his work with his father.

"How did you meet Jesus?" asked Noah.

"I am coming to that," said Levi, laughing. "You see, the market was not busy that morning, although we did not know yet that it was because Jesus was near the town and many people were going to see him. But my father said I could go off and explore a little. He would take care of the people who came to buy things.

"So, he gave me money to get some provisions, and I bought a lot—bread and some good dried fish. Now that I think of it, it's strange that I bought so much. I had no friends with me, like I do today. I'm not sure why I did it. Anyway, I wandered around and ended up following a bunch of people who were hurrying somewhere excitedly. I followed them out of the town and into the countryside. They said that Jesus was nearby and they wanted to go hear him speak.

"I had never heard of Jesus before, but they were so excited that I began to look forward to it."

"How come you had never heard of Jesus?" asked Noah, surprised. "Didn't your mother and father tell you about him?"

"No," said Levi, looking a little irritated. "Why should they?"

Noah opened his mouth to say something—something even more confusing, I'm sure—but I jumped in.

"Did the people say why they wanted to go hear him speak?"

"They just said that they heard he was a great teacher and worker of signs," said Levi. "Soon we saw a large crowd of people on a hillside. Someone I was walking with pointed Jesus out to me. He was higher up the hill, speaking in a loud voice. From where we were, I could hear him speaking, but I could not understand what he was saying. I left the people I had been walking with and went quickly through the crowd, trying to get closer."

Levi paused in his story and looked around. Hannah and Noah and I were waiting for him to continue.

"I think we should head this way," said Levi, pointing and walking.

"So, did you get close to him?" asked Noah.

Levi smiled. "Yes, of course. I am very good at squeezing my way through crowds of people. It is easier to do alone, though. The four of us might have a more difficult time."

"We can do it," I said. "We're good at squeezing, too."

"Well, I headed up the hill, through the crowd, and got very close to where Jesus was. I sat near a group of friendly men that I later found out were his disciples. I could see and hear everything that was going on."

"What was he talking about?" asked Hannah.

Levi sighed. "I wish I could remember! I was paying more attention to the crowds of people that kept coming."

"Did you see him work any miracles?" I asked. "Did he cure anyone?"

Levi stopped walking and stood facing us.

"I did not see him heal anyone who was sick, if that's what you mean. But I saw something else. It was so amazing that you will not believe me when I tell you."

Chapter Five

Levi's Story

"What, Levi? Please tell me! What did you see?" I asked.

"As it got late, I realized that I should start walking back to town. I heard the disciples near me talking to each other. They were saying that the people were going to be stuck in the countryside at nightfall if Jesus did not finish speaking soon and send them away. One of them said that there was nowhere nearby to get provisions, so people would be hungry if they did not have any food left. And probably they did not, because they had been listening to Jesus all day and would have already eaten everything they had brought.

"I heard what they were saying. I felt funny because I actually did have some bread and fish. So, I went over to one of the men and said, 'I have some bread and fish still left, if you want to share it.'"

"That was nice of you, Levi," said Hannah.

"As I was getting it out of my bag, some of the disciples went over to Jesus and started telling him to dismiss the people so they would have time to go find something to eat.

"And Jesus said something strange to them. He said, 'You give them something to eat.'

"So of course they told him they didn't have any bread left, much less enough to feed the whole crowd of people. One of them added, 'There's a boy here who has five loaves and two fish, but what is that for this huge crowd?'"

"Oh!" said Hannah. She had a strange look on her face, like she suddenly understood something.

"Jesus motioned with his hand for me to come over to him. He asked me if I would give

him my bread and fish so he could share it with the crowd. I did not know what to say. He sat there smiling at me, and I was willing to give him anything he asked for, but I could not see how my food would be of any use to the crowd. Even if you divided it all up into pieces, it would not be enough for everyone to get even a tiny bite.

"But I handed him my bag, and he took out the bread and fish and spread the bag on the ground. He laid the bread and fish on the bag and gave thanks to God for the food, like usual. He broke the loaves and the fish into pieces. Then he called his disciples over and had them hold out their mantles. He put some pieces into each of their mantles and told them to go share the food with the crowds.

"The men looked a little embarrassed as they went to bring the food to the people. Each of them was mobbed by people trying to be the first to get a piece of bread. I kept seeing people walking away with a loaf and a piece of fish, or even a couple loaves. I squeezed through a bunch of people who were around the man I had gone to talk to. I finally got up close to him, and he was holding out his mantle, full of bread and fish. Just full!"

"Wow!" said Noah. Wow was right. Now I remembered hearing this story in the Bible. It was the story of the five loaves and two fish. And Levi had *been there.*

Levi stopped talking and stared out into the countryside, but he wasn't looking at the hills. He seemed to be remembering what he had seen that day.

"I got a loaf and began to eat it myself," Levi finally continued. "It took a while for me to realize what had happened, Jesus had done something impossible. He had taken my five loaves and two fish and made them into enough for that entire crowd. *And,* at the end, there were baskets and baskets left over!"

Levi began walking again, and we all walked with him. "So that is why I want to go see Jesus again. He is someone amazing. I want to listen to him teaching, and this time I want to try to understand and remember better what he says."

Chapter Six

Caught in the Storm

After a while, we stopped near a stream to drink and to have something to eat. Levi told us stories of the trips he had taken with his dad. They went all over the place. And his dad let him do all kinds of things!

"It's not fair," I said. "My dad has a cool job, too. He's a carpenter. But he won't let me do anything."

"He's teaching you woodworking," said Hannah.

"No, he's not," I said. "He just wanted to teach me all this baby stuff about safety and really basic stuff about wood. He won't let me *do* anything or *make* anything."

"My father was also like that in the beginning," said Levi. "For a long time I learned about reading the sky and about safety in traveling. Which reminds me!" He jumped to his feet. "We should be going. We should not have sat and talked for so long."

The clouds had turned darker. It had already been cloudy when we set out, but now it looked like a storm was coming.

It got windier, and Levi showed us how to wrap our mantles around our heads and shoulders. He was surprised that we didn't know what to do with them.

As we walked, I saw Levi looking from side to side.

"What are you looking for?" I asked.

"I am trying to remember everything my father taught me about directions," said Levi. He looked like he was thinking hard. "We were supposed to be going southwest, and I think we have been. So we should be near Jotapata. If there is a storm, Jesus will not be teaching out in the countryside. He and all the people will probably go to the town for shelter, and we will, too."

We continued walking and suddenly, without warning, there was a huge flash of lightning and a crack of thunder at the same time.

All of us screamed. The lightning had hit the top of a little hill nearby. I had never seen lightning hit that close!

Then the sky opened and the rain came pouring down, not in drops, but in one solid waterfall, like a bucket being emptied.

"We have to get down somewhere!" said Hannah. "We'll get hit by lightning if we keep standing here."

Flash! Crack! Another bolt of lightning flashed, this time behind us and almost as close as the last one.

Usually I am not afraid of thunderstorms. Noah gets scared, but I don't. I feel safe and secure inside the house, even if the electricity goes out. But now, we were out in the middle of the storm. There was nothing between us and it. I was definitely afraid.

We looked around, trying to see somewhere safe to go. But it was raining so hard.

Levi walked a little way ahead, but he didn't know the area any better than we did, so I didn't think he had much chance of finding anything. Noah was so scared that he pressed up against me.

Flash! Crack! Another lightning bolt struck, and this time it was so close that I could smell the burnt shrub that had been hit. Noah and I both jumped, and I hugged him closer. I could tell he was crying.

"Hey!" we heard Levi call from a little way in front of us. Then he turned around and motioned with his hand. "Hey! Come down here. There's a little place for us."

We all hurried over to him and saw that there was a large rock at the base of a hill. It stuck out a little over a dip in the land. The rock was big enough to get under, so we all sat down in a row, with our backs against the rock. It didn't keep out the rain completely, but it felt safer.

It seemed like the storm kept up for hours. I was so soaked, I was shivering. We tried to huddle close to each other.

Finally, the rain was just falling lightly and there was no more thunder.

Levi pulled his bag off his shoulder. He opened it and pulled out a loaf of bread, which he passed to me.

"Thanks, Levi," I said. "I was afraid everything would be wet!"

"No, this is well-oiled leather," said Levi. "My father gets good leather from a tanner in Gadara, and my mother made it for me."

I broke off a chunk and passed the loaf to Noah, who did the same. Hannah had the rest. We also ate cheese and dried figs. (They were really good!)

For a while we just ate and no one talked. The rain finally stopped.

Then Hannah spoke.

"Um, Levi, do you have any idea where we are?"

Chapter Seven

Walking in the Dark

Levi stood up and looked around. Then he looked at us and shrugged.

"I will tell you the truth," said Levi. "I am not completely sure if I still know the right way to Jotapata."

"What will we do when it gets dark if we cannot find the town?" I said.

"I am sure we will find a farm to stay at."

"*Completely* sure?" asked Hannah.

"I am sorry. I should have said *I hope* we will find a farm to stay at. Otherwise we will be very uncomfortable tonight."

We all got up and started off. It was no fun walking in our wet clothes.

At one point, the setting sun showed through the clouds a tiny bit.

"Oh, that is good," said Levi. "We are still heading southwest."

We walked and walked. Soon it began to get dark. I was so tired that I was just about to say we should stop, when suddenly I saw something up ahead. Something really scary.

It wasn't totally dark yet, and I had caught sight of a large bumpy monster-looking thing not far from us. It looked kind of like a dragon or a monster-sized lizard. It wasn't part of the rocky ground, because I could see it had legs.

"What. Is. *That*?" I whispered.

"What?" "Where?" everyone asked.

I pointed and whispered, "There!"

None of us moved. The thing stayed still, too.

"Do you think it saw us?" Hannah whispered.

"Are there dinosaurs around here?" asked Noah.

Suddenly there was a loud laugh. I jumped and was ready to run, but then I realized it was Levi laughing.

I wanted to tell him to be quiet or he'd wake the monster, but he didn't seem afraid at all.

"You all are so funny!" he said. "Do you not see what that is?"

"No, what is it? Some kind of Galilean monster?" I said, annoyed.

"Monster? You are too much!" At this point Levi was practically rolling on the ground with laughter. "That is a grape vine!"

"What?" we all said together. Okay, I had never seen a grape vine, but I just knew there was no way *that* was a grape vine!

"Come over here," said Levi. So we walked over to it, staying behind him. Up close, it looked like dead plants. It was just a row of wrinkled trunks and some branches cut off. I guess we just had to believe him that it was a grape vine.

We were still marveling over the weirdness of it when I noticed Levi stepping away and looking all around. Was he worried about monsters after all?

"What are you looking for now, Levi?"

"Well, we wandered into this vineyard, so I'm looking for the watchtower or the vinedresser's house. At least it would be somewhere to sleep."

"Is this the town we were going to?" asked Noah.

"It should be very close to Jotapata. The vineyards would be within sight of the town, I am sure."

"Yay!" said Noah.

We walked along a little farther and finally Noah spotted the watchtower, a tall structure from which a man could keep watch over the vineyard. We went toward it and then Levi saw the house.

Before we got near the house, though, we heard someone yell, "Hail! Who goes there? Show yourself!"

At the same time we saw a man with a lantern. He was walking toward us.

Chapter Eight

Eli and Abigail

"Hello!" responded Levi. "We got lost in the storm. We are travelers in need of hospitality. Can you help us?"

"Well, well," said the man as he caught sight of us in the light of his lantern. "Four children. Yes, please come with me. My wife will be very happy to welcome you and give you something to eat. We get few visitors and we have no children, so lost travelers will be very welcome."

In the dark, I couldn't tell much about this man except that he was big and tall. Once we reached the house and went in, I saw he was mostly bald but had a full beard that was partly brown and partly white. He was smiling and seemed to mean what he said about being happy to have visitors.

"Abigail, my love, come! We have guests!" he called.

A woman came from behind a curtain. She looked older than Mom. Her long brown hair was partly white in the front. As soon as she saw us, her face broke into a big smile. Then she looked upset.

"Oh, you are all soaked to the skin! Eli, quick, put more wood on the fire and fill my kettle. These poor children need dry clothes and something warm to drink."

Abigail started bustling around, bringing us closer to the fire, and unwrapping our wet mantles. She asked our names and told us not to worry, soon we would be dry and comfortable.

"Oh, and what shall we do for some clothes for them to wear? Eli, bring me your good tunic and the one that you tore the other day. Those will do for the older boys."

She helped Hannah take off her mantle. "I have something you can wear, dear," she said. "But the little one might have to make do with a blanket, I'm afraid," she said, looking at Noah.

I got to wear the tunic Eli had torn, with a mantle wrapped around me on top. Noah didn't have to wear a blanket after all. Abigail found another old tunic. I think it was hers, but I didn't ask because I didn't want Noah to feel bad about wearing a girl's tunic. All of us had to pull up and tie the clothes around our waists because they were all way too big.

Abigail and Eli were just about the nicest people we had ever met. After getting us warm and dry, Abigail prepared food for us. And they insisted that we keep eating until we couldn't eat any more. While we ate, Abigail went and washed out our clothes and hung them up to dry.

"You must all be exhausted," said Abigail.

"Well, perhaps they would like to relax by the fire for a while and talk," said Eli.

"No, Eli, that is what *you* would like them to do," said Abigail. "We can hear their story in the morning. Now is the time for sleep."

Boy, was I glad to hear that. It had been such a long walk to Jotapata, and I was really tired. Noah was leaning sideways as he slowly fell asleep where he sat.

"Eli, put some of our winter bedding down on top of these rushes. They can sleep here near the fire."

Eli put down some mats that looked like they were made of straw. Then he laid blankets on top. I lay down next to Noah, with Hannah on the other side of him and Levi next to me. It was very comfortable.

The last thing I remember before I fell asleep was listening to Abigail say quietly to Eli, "Look how beautiful they are as they sleep. How I wish we had some children of our own."

Chapter Nine

Mix-Ups

The next morning, I woke up and immediately thought of going to see what the grape vine monster looked like in the daylight. I sat up and pushed back my blanket. It was definitely daylight out. It seemed as sunny as noon, and my stomach felt like it should be lunchtime, too.

"Good morning, Caleb," Eli said quietly. He was rolling up the blankets and the mat that had been next to me.

"Good morning," I said. I looked and saw Hannah and Noah still sleeping.

"What time is it? Where's Levi?" I asked.

"He just left. When he woke up and saw how late he had slept, he said he needed to meet his father in town."

"Yeah, he was really worried about that when we got lost in the storm yesterday."

"You must be hungry, Caleb. Come outside and have something to eat. We will let your sister and brother sleep."

Abigail gave me a bowl of some mushy stuff. She said it was barley. Usually I wouldn't have wanted to eat it, but I was so hungry, I could have eaten anything. Then she gave me some bread with honey.

After I ate, Eli showed me some of the vineyard, and I saw the "monster" that had looked so scary the night before. There were rows of them, actually. In the daylight, it was more obvious that they were plants. But I still had a hard time believing they were grape vines! Eli said the vines were dormant at this time of year. Later he would have a lot of work pruning the vines and harvesting the grapes.

I got to go up in the watchtower, too. I could see really far in all directions.

"So, is that Jotapata?" I asked, looking over the vineyard and the house to a town I could see close by.

"No, that is Cana. You cannot see Jotapata from here," said Eli.

"What?" I asked. "So how far away is it? Levi thought the vineyard would be very close to the town."

"It *is* very close to the town," said Eli, looking puzzled. "To the town of Cana, which you can see right there."

"Cana? Did you tell Levi that the town is called Cana?"

"No, I do not remember that he asked me. He just said he must go find his father in town, so Abigail gave him something to eat on the way."

"Eli, I think Levi is not going to find his father there. His father said to meet him in Jotapata—that is where we were walking to when we got caught in the storm."

"Oh, that is not good. I think we should go to town ourselves and find the boy."

Eli went to tell Abigail that we were going.

"Your brother and sister are awake and are eating now. Abigail will look after them," said Eli.

It wasn't a very long walk to Cana. We walked quickly, and I told Eli about everything that had happened the day before. How we had started out from Sogane to Jotapata in the morning, but had arrived in the vineyard when it was dark.

"Yes, Sogane is closer to Jotapata. You should have arrived before two or three hours had passed," said Eli.

When we got into Cana, we went toward the market area, because that's where Levi would have gone to find his dad.

"Do you see him?" asked Eli, looking around.

The marketplace was not very full, so I could see pretty quickly that he was not there.

"What kind of merchant is Levi's father?" asked Eli. "Do you know what he sells?"

"Well, he had some different kinds of small metal pots. And some spices," I said.

"Hmm. He might have gone to the street with the metalsmiths."

"Oh, I remember that his father said to stay in Jotapata with the coppersmith there!"

We walked down the street, away from the open area of the market. We passed a few side streets, and then Eli turned left. I was getting worried about where Levi had gone. I thought about how he would feel about his dad not finding him. Maybe Levi was still looking around

Cana for him. Maybe he hadn't realized yet that this wasn't Jotapata. It didn't sound like he had been here before.

We found the coppersmith of Cana. Eli seemed to be friends with him. They smiled as they greeted each other.

"Shalom, Eli," the coppersmith said as soon as he saw us. "I was going to visit you today!"

"Shalom, my friend. Here I am—I have saved you the trip!" said Eli. "But why would you come to my vineyard? I have no grapes for you, and you have no copper work for me."

"Ah, I was not going to bring you any copper, but a message," said the man. "A boy named Levi was here. He said he had enjoyed your hospitality last night. He asked me to send his deepest thanks and farewell to you."

"Yes, I suspected he would come to you. He was indeed my guest last night."

"Excuse me!" I interrupted. "Can you please tell us where he is? It's very important!"

"Certainly, son. He left not long ago to travel to Jotapata. He said to tell you that, in case his father came looking for him."

Chapter Ten

Comings and Goings

"Back to Jotapata? How long would that take?" I asked.

"Oh, it is now almost the seventh hour," said the man, looking up at the sky. "So he should be there around the tenth hour. If he doesn't run into any trouble."

"What should we do, Eli?" I asked.

"I do not think it is a good idea for Levi to go to Jotapata. His father will be looking for him and maybe has already realized he is not there. If he goes elsewhere to look for him, they will miss each other again."

"I could go after him," I said. "How long ago did he leave?"

"Ah . . . a short time ago. I don't remember exactly," said the coppersmith.

"Which way is Jotapata?" I asked.

The man pointed and I started to run off.

"Caleb! Wait!" said Eli.

I turned and saw Eli wave goodbye to the coppersmith. Then he walked toward me.

"Come, I will walk with you to show you the road to follow. Then you can run ahead because I cannot go as quickly as you can."

We went down the street and he pointed out the road. It went through an area with trees and up and down a hill. I couldn't see it after that.

"Do not go too far," said Eli. "If you do not find him before an hour has passed, come back. If you do find him, tell him that I will have a message sent to Jotapata and to Sogane, and we will find his father. I will go right now and find someone who needs to make a trip that way."

I started off running. When I began to get tired, I walked quickly for a while, then ran again for a while. After the first hill, there was another one. And another one after that.

Just when I was afraid that I was on the wrong road, or that Levi had decided to run all the way to Jotapata, I saw him in the distance.

"Levi!" I called, but he was too far away to hear me.

Now I ran fast, and the next time I shouted his name, he turned around.

"Wait!" I yelled.

By the time I caught up with him, I was out of breath.

"What are you doing, Caleb? Did you not get my message? I must go back to find my father." Levi looked angry.

"We got it . . . but Eli says . . . to come back . . . He will send . . . messages to Jotapata . . . and Sogane."

"*Eli* says? My *father* said to meet him in Jotapata. Today! I must get there soon or he will not know what happened to me."

"No, wait, Levi." I tried to think what to say to make him understand. "I think it would be better for you to come back."

"You do not understand, Caleb!" said Levi. "What will my father think when I have failed to meet him? He will think I am too young to come with him on his trips. He will say that I do not know well what he has taught me about traveling." He paused and then said more quietly, "He will be so disappointed in me!"

I didn't know what to say. In one way, he was right. His father might think all that. And I could see why Levi wanted to try to be where his father had told him to be. But Eli was right, too. It would not be good for Levi and his father to go back and forth looking for each other.

"I know what you mean, Levi," I said. "I would feel the same way if it were my father."

"So you see why I have to go?"

"No, you have to stay here and let a message be sent. Otherwise it could just happen all over again. I think your father will understand that you did your best in the storm. And you were with the three of us who don't know anything about finding our way."

Levi looked like he was about to disagree.

"And even your father can make mistakes," I said. "Remember how he said to bring the mantle because it looked like it might rain. He didn't know how bad that storm was going to be."

"But my father will say I can only come to the local markets and help him pack for his trips. I want to travel with him, to meet people, and to see new places. I do not want to stay home!" Levi said.

"But even if that happens, it won't be forever. After a while, he will let you travel with him again."

Levi sighed. He looked down the road to Jotapata, and back again at Cana. "You are right, Caleb. I will just explain what happened and then do what my father says."

We walked slowly back to town. As we entered the area with the trees (Levi said they were olive trees), we met a man with a pack on his back. He walked up to us and told us that he had to go to Jotapata on business, so Eli had asked him to take the message. If he did not find Levi's father, he would send a message to Sogane and leave messages with others, so that anyone who saw Levi's father would let him know where his son was.

The sun was already low in the sky by the time we got back to the vineyard. Eli took all of us up in the watchtower. We watched the amazing red and purple sunset. Levi didn't even seem to see it. He looked very worried about his father.

Chapter Eleven

Abigail's Story

After dinner we sat around talking and eating walnuts.

"Tell us your story, please, Abigail," said Hannah. "You said there was something that we would be happy to hear."

"We already told her *your* story, Levi," said Noah.

"I hope you don't mind," said Hannah. "Abigail really enjoyed it. She said she had a story to tell, too, but she wouldn't tell us until you were here."

Levi just shrugged his shoulders.

"I know you are worried, Levi," said Abigail. "I hope this will cheer you up a little.

"My story happened at a wedding. It was a lovely spring wedding, and the courtyard of the house was filled with flowers and their scent. It seemed that most of the people of Galilee had been invited!

"When the wedding celebration was about half over, I noticed a woman who wasn't from our town. I went over to introduce myself, and I found out that her name was Mary and she was from Nazareth. That's a little town south of here."

"Nazareth!" said Hannah. "That's where Jesus is from!"

"Yes, that is right," said Abigail. "Mary and her son, Jesus, were at the wedding."

"How far away is Nazareth?" I asked.

"No!" said Levi. "Never mind how far away it is. We are not going there."

Abigail laughed. "Yes, I agree. Nazareth is not much to look at anyway.

"As I was saying, Mary had been invited to the wedding, along with her son and some of

his friends. I don't think his friends even knew the bride or the groom, but that's how weddings are—many people come from all around to join the celebration. They were all enjoying themselves.

"Then it happened! They *ran out* of wine!"

Abigail looked like she was telling us something horrible. It didn't seem so terrible to me. I mean, they could just go buy some more or give people something else to drink.

"Didn't they give everyone beer or soda or something?" asked Noah.

"What?" said Abigail.

"Nothing. Never mind," I said. "Couldn't they go buy some more?"

"No, they had no more money. It costs a lot to have a wedding. They had not planned well for so many people, and they ran out. There was still plenty of food, but how embarrassing to run out of wine!

"I heard the headwaiter talking about it to one of the servants who had been refilling people's cups with wine. Right after that, Mary walked by, the woman I told you about. I told her what I had overheard. She said she had an idea of what to do.

"I followed her as she walked over to where her son, Jesus, was sitting. She told him that they had run out of wine. I waited to see what he would say. He did not look like a rich man, but perhaps he had a large store of wine he could share.

"What he said was, 'What does that have to do with me? My hour has not yet come.'"

"What does that mean?" I asked.

"I was not sure myself. He certainly *seemed*

to be saying that he could not or would not help the couple.

"But Mary had faith that he would help. She just turned and said to the servant nearby, 'Do whatever he tells you.'

"The servant went over to Jesus and waited for his instructions. I was just as surprised as he was when Jesus told him to fill the large stone jars with water. The servant got some other servants to help because there were six jars and they were very large. Almost as tall as you, Noah. After they had finished, the servant went to tell Jesus that they had done as he said. Jesus told him to take some out of the jar and bring it to the head waiter.

"Now I was very puzzled. Why would Jesus want the head waiter to see or drink the water? Was he trying to tell him that it was his fault that there was no more wine?

"I was curious what the waiter would do, so I watched as the servant gave him the water. You will never guess what happened."

"What?" asked Levi. "What happened?" He was really into the story after all.

"It was no longer water," said Abigail in a quiet voice. "It had turned into wine. All those jars were filled with very good wine. It was even better than what we had been drinking before, the headwaiter said. There was plenty of wine for the people to continue to celebrate the couple's wedding."

"Wow!" said Noah.

Now I understood why Abigail thought Levi would like this story. It was so much like his!

"I know it sounds unbelievable, but it is true. There are many here in Cana who were there," said Abigail.

"I believe you," said Levi. "Thank you for telling me the story."

Eli had been quiet this whole time. He just sat, cracking walnuts and smiling at Abigail.

Now he looked at Levi.

"Son, sleep in peace tonight. We will find your father tomorrow. If not, we will keep looking until we do. And even if it happened that we never found him, you have a place here with us. So do not worry."

The next morning, right after breakfast, Levi, Hannah, Noah, and I went into town with Abigail. Eli had been up before dawn, Abigail said, and had gone ahead of us.

We were walking through the market on the way to the coppersmith's house. Suddenly I saw Eli rushing toward us.

"Levi!" he called. "Your father is here! He was afraid you were lost in the storm. He is very happy to have found you."

"Yay!" Noah cheered, jumping up and down.

Levi was smiling big as he hurried toward Eli. Together they quickly went ahead of us.

"I hope his dad isn't mad," said Hannah.

"It didn't sound like it," I said.

"We can take our time," said Abigail, "so that Levi can have time with his father before we get there. Come, I will point out the house where Jesus turned water into wine."

A couple streets down, she pointed.

"That is the house—you can see the entrance to the courtyard through there."

"We *have* to go see the courtyard," I said. "We'll be right back, Abigail."

Noah ran ahead of us and we went through the open door in the wall of the courtyard.

"Look!" said Noah. "Do you think those are the jars?"

"They're huge," said Hannah. "As tall as Noah."

We started to walk over to look at them more closely. Suddenly we were moving in slow motion, and then we were standing under the branches of the old willow tree near the garden of our house.

Chapter Twelve

Another Miracle

"Oh!" said Noah. "I didn't want to come back!"

The last time we had come back from a trip to the time of Jesus, it had taken only a couple of minutes. I mean, we were there for two nights, but when we came back, it was only about two minutes after we had left.

Hannah wanted to make sure that the same thing had happened this time, so she went in the house to find Mom. She came right back out.

"Mom just said hi and asked if I'd help her

make grilled cheese sandwiches for lunch," said Hannah.

"Well, that means they didn't miss us," I said.

Hannah went back into the house, and Noah and I sat under the tree.

"That was fun," said Noah. "But we still didn't see Jesus."

"Yeah," I said. "I hope we get a chance to go again."

"Do you think we will, Caleb?"

"I think so," I said. And then, even though I knew Hannah couldn't hear me, I whispered, "We just need to figure out how to make it happen again!"

Noah and I talked all afternoon about what we could try to do to make ourselves go back in time.

The next day was Sunday and I heard something that made me forget about that for a while.

At Mass, Father Joe talked about the feast day we were celebrating. It's called Corpus Christi. (That means, "the Body of Christ.")

"If you've ever wished you could see a miracle happen, today is your lucky day," he said. "What is about to happen in this church is so amazing you will scarcely believe it."

I sat up at that and looked at Noah. His eyes were wide open like he didn't want to miss the miracle when it happened.

"You have read in the Bible about the miracles Jesus performed during his lifetime," Father Joe continued. "He healed people, multiplied the loaves and fish, calmed a storm, turned water into wine!"

I looked at Hannah and she smiled back at me.

"But none of those can compare with what is about to happen here today in just a few minutes. A piece of round, flat bread and a cup of wine will become the Body and Blood of Jesus. They will look like the same bread and wine, and even taste and smell the same. But they will no longer be bread and wine. They will be changed into Jesus.

"At the time of Jesus, bread and wine were very basic kinds of food. They were eaten every day. They are very ordinary things, but at Mass something amazing happens to them. It's happening today! Jesus is coming here today! We should be so excited. How can anyone say that Mass is boring or that they don't get anything out of it? They get Jesus!"

Wow, I thought to myself. Of course, I learned all about that when I made my first Communion, but sometimes I forget. This Sunday, when I was kneeling in the pew after Communion, I really *got* it, if you know what I mean.

I told Jesus "thank you" for coming to me. Then I just stayed there, feeling happy that Jesus was with me. I didn't talk to him. I just enjoyed his company.

After church I had an idea. Maybe it came from Jesus, although I didn't hear him say anything. I was thinking about how Jesus used that ordinary bread to give us himself and also about how he used the water and turned it into wine. And how he took one boy's lunch and made it into food for thousands of people. It made me think of my dad making things out of wood. A piece of wood is very ordinary and boring. But it can be made into fun and wonderful and useful things.

When we got back from church, I walked over to my dad.

"Dad?" I said. "Can I try again to learn woodworking? I don't mind if you teach me the boring parts first."

My dad smiled. "Sure, Caleb. I'm glad you are willing to try again. I did realize afterward that I could have started out in a better way. I'll try to show you *why* the basic stuff is important. And we can start one project from scratch, so you can help me through all the stages. How does that sound?"

"That's great, Dad, thanks!"

Where Is It in the Bible?

In the Bible, there are four Gospels, which each tell about Jesus in a different way. The story of how Jesus multiplied the loaves and the fish is in all four Gospels, but only one of them, the Gospel according to John, gives the important bit of information that it was a boy who gave Jesus the five loaves and two fish that he used to feed the whole crowd. Here is the story:

After this Jesus went to the other side of the Sea of Galilee, also called the Sea of

Tiberias. A large crowd kept following him, because they saw the signs that he was doing for the sick. Jesus went up the mountain and sat down there with his disciples. Now the Passover, the festival of the Jews, was near. When he looked up and saw a large crowd coming toward him, Jesus said to Philip, "Where are we to buy bread for these people to eat?" He said this to test him, for he himself knew what he was going to do. Philip answered him, "Six months' wages would not buy enough bread for each of them to get a little." One of his disciples, Andrew, Simon Peter's brother, said to him, "There is a boy here who has five barley loaves and two fish. But what are they among so many people?" Jesus said, "Make the people sit down." Now there was a great deal of grass in the place; so they sat down, about five thousand in all. Then Jesus took the loaves, and when he had given thanks, he distributed them to those who were seated; so also the fish, as much as they wanted. When they were satisfied, he told his disciples, "Gather up the fragments left over, so that nothing may be lost." So they gathered them up, and from the fragments of the five barley loaves, left by those who had eaten, they filled twelve baskets (John 6:1–13).

The story about the wedding at Cana is only told in one of the Gospels—the Gospel according to John. Here it is:

On the third day there was a wedding in Cana of Galilee, and the mother of Jesus was there. Jesus and his disciples had also been invited to the wedding. When the wine gave out, the mother of Jesus said to him, 'They have no wine.' And Jesus said to her, 'Woman, what concern is that to you and to me? My hour has not yet come.' His mother said to the servants, 'Do whatever he tells you.' Now standing there were six stone water-jars for the Jewish rites of purification, each holding twenty or thirty gallons. Jesus said to them, 'Fill the jars with water.' And they filled them up to the brim. He said to them, 'Now draw some out, and take it to the chief steward.' So they took it. When the steward tasted the water that had become wine, and did not know where it came from (though the servants who had drawn the water knew), the steward called the bridegroom and said to him, 'Everyone serves the good wine first, and then the inferior wine after the guests have become drunk. But you have kept the good wine until now.' Jesus did this, the first of his signs, in Cana of Galilee, and revealed his glory; and his disciples believed in him (John 2:1–11).